Billy Two Hawks

The Train

Julian Ashbourn

ISBN 10: 1724986147
ISBN 13: 978-1724986146

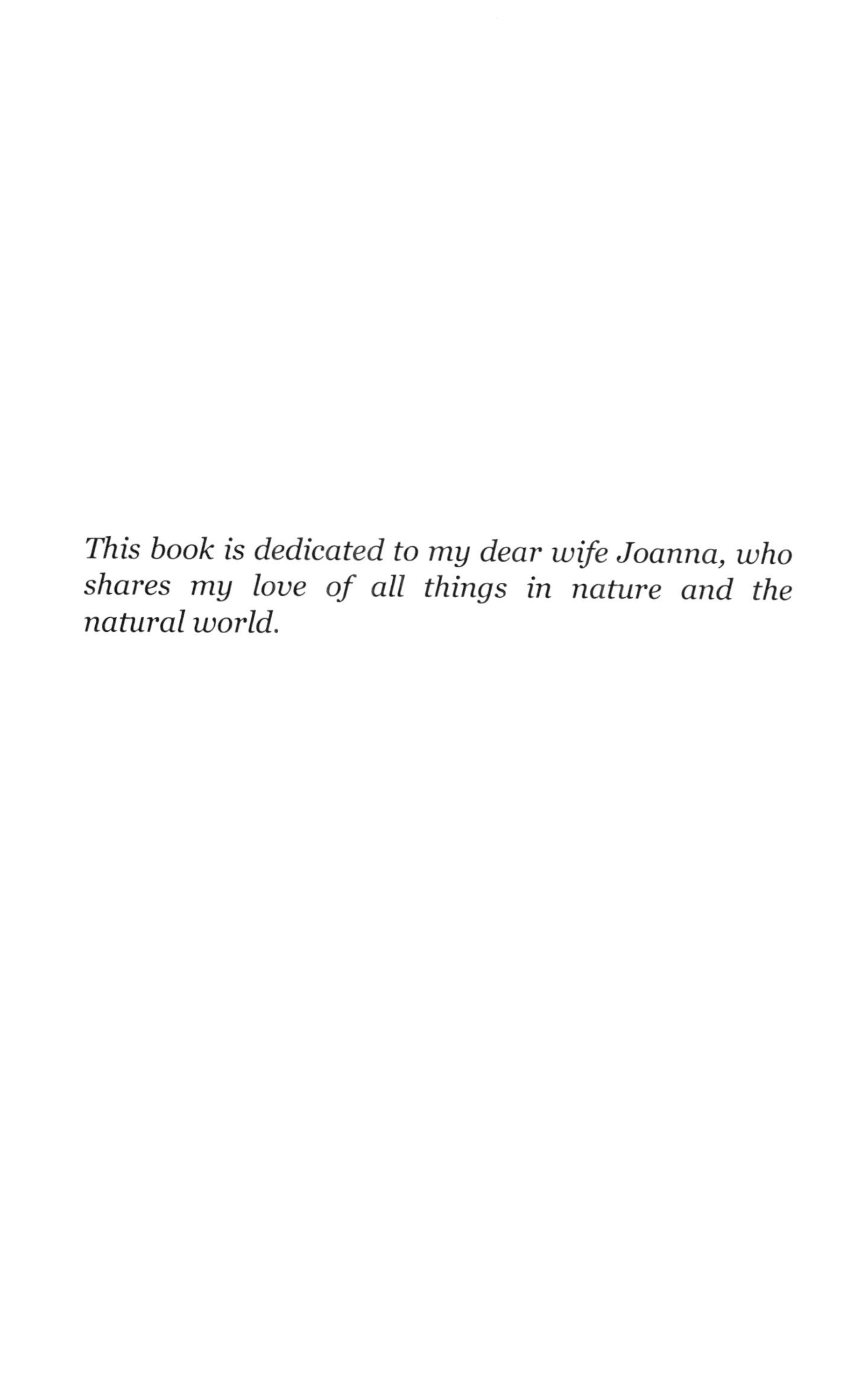

This book is dedicated to my dear wife Joanna, who shares my love of all things in nature and the natural world.

Contents

1. Introduction

Tānisi. My name is Billy Two Hawks; Nîso Kêhkêhk, and I am a Cree Indian. I live on the Bridgewater Reserve which is just a kilometre from Pinehouse Lake on route 914 in Northern Saskatchewan, my home province, north by north west from Lac La Ronge. Float planes used to land on the lake and occasionally still do. There is a little wooden jetty which juts out just far enough for them to come in alongside and tie up to a large wooden pole which was sunk there for the purpose, some years ago. Nowadays there is a small airstrip cleared alongside the main stretch of the lake where light aircraft may land. This, in turn, leads on to a road which branches, one way leading to the Bridgewater Reserve and the other back to route 914. Sometimes, such as in an emergency, this air link is extremely important and offers a life-line to the outside world. But mostly, our

Reserve is quiet and peaceful, up here among the lakes and forests. In addition to the main lake, there are dozens of smaller lakes, many of them interconnected and some of which only have names given to them by my ancestors. It would be possible, with a canoe, to travel for many miles among this network of beautiful lakes, only stopping occasionally for a section of portage. I love it here and would never wish to live anywhere else in this world. This is where my soul is bound to the earth.

I often rise early and wander through the beautiful pine forests, sometimes following a trail and sometimes not, until I come to some idyllic little spot by the side of one of the lakes. Here I will clear a space and lay down upon the soft forest floor, among the pine needles and grass, looking out across the still water, its surface like a mirror, reflecting the tall, green trees along its banks. As the sun climbs in the sky, sâkâstew, I reflect upon many things. About life up here in the north, compared to life in the cities. About how I shall live my life and my own codes of ethics and humanity. And, especially, how I relate to the natural world around me. A world full of beauty and examples of the miracles of nature; every creature, every tree and the cohesiveness of it all, up here where few humans set foot, except my own people living on the Reserve. But few of them venture as far as I do, deep into the forests and along the shores of the myriad of small lakes, with all their glorious natural beauty. Walking through the forests fills my heart with gladness and makes me feel pleased to be alive. Laying here on the soft carpet of pine needles, looking out over the lake, I sometimes feel that Misimanito, the Great Spirit is laying here with me. It is a warm feeling, as I gradually become absorbed into nature and am at one with my surroundings. Looking towards the sky, I see a lone buzzard, circling slowly and drifting with the thermal currents coming up from the lake. He gives a little cry and I send him telepathic messages of goodwill. Red squirrels chatter around me, slowly becoming closer and closer as their curiosity overcomes their natural shyness. "Tānisi", I call to them softly and they sit up on their hind legs and look straight into my eyes. We are brothers, here in the forest which we both love so much.

And I have larger brothers here. The black bears and, very occasionally, grizzly bears roam through these northern forests. Several of the black bears have come to recognise me and I, in turn, strive to recognise them and give them names. They are happy to coexist with me here and we often cross paths and have an occasional little chat. They are also curious and sometimes come right up to me, examining me closely before moving on. They never cease to make me smile and I love them all. I also like to stay out in the forest in the evenings and sometimes well into the night. They become a different world then, full of interesting sounds and shadows as the moonlight finds its way through every natural aperture. Tipiskāwipisim, the big yellow moon, follows me wherever I roam and seems always to be watching over me, ensuring that I come to no harm. Sitting here in the moonlight, I here the most beautiful sound that I know of on this Earth. The sound of two or more wolves, calling to each other through the forest. Their beautiful voices can carry for miles and they recognise each other by voice, thus being able to pinpoint their precise location. They are wonderful creatures who exercise their own code of living, with every individual understanding his own responsibilities within the extended family group. I sometimes catch a fleeting glimpse of them through the trees, but they are shy and do not come close. I understand and send them telepathic messages of love and goodwill. The Great Spirit seems to guide me on my wandering through the wilderness, revealing secrets of the natural world that few have seen, or would understand. I can never tire of just being here, absorbed into forest as a part of the miracle of nature.

And so, this is my world. It is a beautiful world that I never wish to leave. However, sometimes, fate decrees that I must leave it, briefly, in order to be of service to my fellow Canadians. These rare excursions from my everyday life occur when the Royal Canadian Mounted Police 'F' division, have an unsolved crime which they believe I may be able to help them with. Naturally, there is a list of such crimes which remain outstanding but, sometimes, there is one which they believe may be of particular significance, especially if it is likely to stretch across Provinces.

In such circumstances, I usually meet with my special contact, Detective Sergeant Robert Conwy, at the Redlands Café on Preston Avenue in Saskatoon, just before the road continues on to the University of Saskatchewan campus. The café is owned by Grace Billing who, by now, has grown accustomed to us meeting there and, if available, taking the back table. The waitress, Rosie Hadder has also come to know us quite well and, once our order is taken, leaves us in peace. They seem to sense that our meetings are important, although they have no idea who we really are.

Bob Conwy reports to Chief Superintendent Stuart Grant at Saskatoon, although the main centre for the RCMP is in Dewdney Avenue, Regina where Superintendent Colin Henley and Commander William Tavistock liaise with the division at Saskatoon. I am full of praise and respect for the Royal Canadian Mounted Police as they have a vast area to cover, within which a myriad of ethnic groups have become established. They do a wonderful job and I have always found them to be courteous and fair as they liaise with this mixed bag of citizens who come under the umbrella of Canadians. On the

Bridgewater Reserve, where I live, we are a small, self-governing community who undertake our own law enforcement. Some other reserves work in partnership with the RCMP and, yet others, are completely policed by the RCMP. Across Canada, there are Germans, Finns, French, British, Russian, Chinese, Japanese, Somalis, Indians and many others. Theirs is a complex and difficult task, with many layers of crime, from domestic violence and robbery to terrorist activities and manipulation of the young. This is why I respect them greatly and am always prepared to help with anything that I can.

I am not a professional private detective and will not work for money or reward of any kind. Furthermore, I insist upon anonymity and ask that my name is not used, or even known, except to those within the force who I have mentioned. The RCMP kindly provide me with a credit card and a mobile phone while I am working on an assignment. This allows me to travel and keep in communication with them. My only other tools are a miniature LED torch and a multi-purpose tool which includes pliers, a screwdriver, two knife blades, a saw blade, a bottle opener and a small pointed shaft. This all folds up into a small pouch which I wear on my belt. Usually, I am to be found on the Reserve where I stay with my aunt, Marie Naytowheh. I was once married, to the most beautiful and sweet natured girl names Sooleawa. I loved Soolie like no man has ever loved a woman but, during a particularly bad winter, some years back now, Soolie contracted a virus and, within a few days, she deteriorated quickly and I lost her. She died while holding my hand at night and breathing gently. She gave me a last smile and then slipped away. We had only been married for three years and I was devastated. For a month or two afterwards, I could not speak and it took quite a while before I could resume a normal life. I will never marry again. Sooleawa's spirit walks with me and I often find myself speaking to her, or asking her opinion about some small thing or another. One day, I will cross the big lake and will meet with her again on the other side. But, until that day, I must continue with my wanderings. No, I shall never marry again.

However, my aunt Marie is very understanding of my situation, including my occasional absence for, sometimes, several weeks at a time, if I am working with my friends from the RCMP. She does not know what I do, but trusts in me that, whatever I am doing, it is for the common good. She never asks about the details, bless her, but her eyes show an unspoken understanding of my work. She is the most important person in my life now as, although there is a community centre on the Bridgewater Reserve, I rarely socialise with others. I prefer to take some water and a little food, and wander off into the wilderness, often for two or three days at a time. It is there that my heart was slowly healed after loosing

Sooleawa and it is only there that I feel really at peace with the world and with life in general.

It was when returning home after just such a sojourn that my aunt Marie informed me that my friend Bob had left a message for me. I was to meet with him at the café the next day at 14.00. Aunt Marie had no idea which café or where it was, and never questioned me about such matters. She is an unusual, loving aunt and my best friend in this world.

I have an old Suzuki jeep which, in spite of its high mileage, continues to serve me well, and which I maintain myself. Whenever the opportunity arises, I gather together some more spares for it and therefore keep it running in very good order. I call my jeep Kanti, after an enigmatic friend of my aunt.

And so, that afternoon, I prepared Kanti for the long trip south and my aunt Marie prepared some food and water to pack into a box for me for the journey. That night, I slept little, but watched the okinānis, the seven stars, from my window and thought of the Great Spirit and the wonder of the universe and our beautiful land.

2. The Body

The journey south, down route 914 and on to route 2, through Prince Albert and on to route 11 down to Saskatoon, is a long one and I was leased to stop at Duck Lake, just south of Prince Albert for a break. The town of Duck Lake has its own history, but I like to visit the Blessed Sacrament Roman Catholic Church, which sits in beautiful grounds where I can sit for a while and have my refreshments. It also has a gas station where I can fill Kanti up, and then, we are both ready to continue our journey.

I arrive at the Redlands Café a little early, and, after greeting Mrs Billing and Rosie, take a seat quietly at the back table. They know that I will be joined in due course by Bob Conwy and then we shall place our order. After a while, Bob, a man of medium build with a moustache and dancing eyes, came quietly in and sat down opposite me. Rosie immediately followed him to our table. "And what will you gentlemen have today?" she asked with a smile. "The usual" grinned Bob, "Two coffees and two of your lovely omelettes with ham and cheese, please". Rosie disappeared and Bob leaned over towards me. His expression became very serious. "We are in trouble with this one Billy" he said quietly. "We are liaising with our colleagues in Alberta over what we first thought was a simple murder, but now we are not so sure". He looked behind him and then continued. "We are pursuing our usual line of enquiries but suspect that there is something else going on in the background. Your particular style of independent investigation may be of help here". I looked at Bill directly and asked, "Who was the dead man?". "It was an RCMP detective by the name of Roger Smythe, from the Alberta section. They believe that he had uncovered some sort of organised crime, possibly related to the Canadian Pacific company". Bob paused as Rosie brought our coffees to the table. "Thank you Rosie" I said quietly. Bob continued; "The body was found in the engineering works at Calgary, partly hidden under a rack of parts". I sipped at my coffee and thought for a few moments. "Why the Canadian Pacific company?" I asked. "Surely they would not be a party to any organised crime". "Maybe not intentionally" replied Bob, "But it could be that some of their employees were involved in some sort of scheme". "What scheme?" I asked. "Well, Smythe was part of the narcotics division". "So they had the perfect distribution system with the railway" I suggested. "That's right. Bring the merchandise in by sea at somewhere like Searsport or Saint John and, within days, you have it spread right across the country, from Montreal to Vancouver". Bob took a sip of his coffee. I thought for a minute or two as Rosie appeared with our omelettes. "Bon appetite" she said smiling and disappeared to the other tables.

I started on my omelette. "But why the engineering works?" I asked. "The whole operation could have been managed at Saint John and the goods shipped as ordinary freight packages without raising any suspicion along the route". "That's what's been troubling us" said Bob. "It doesn't seem to make sense, but what else could it be, given Smythe's involvement and the fact that they were prepared to kill him in order to put the lid on it". I sipped my coffee again. "It has to be something to do with the locomotives" I whispered, almost subconsciously. "You mean a bomb?" asked Bob. "There would be no point. It would hardly do any damage except when the train was in the station, so why not take the bomb straight to the station?". He had a point. "So what would you like me to do?" I asked. "Well, I have a friend in Alberta, Superintendent George Penning, he is willing to meet you privately and discuss the situation with you from their perspective. He doesn't know who you are, except that your name is Billy, but I told him that you can be trusted and that is good enough for him. After all, they would like to get this thing settled. In the meantime, we shall continue to cooperate with the Alberta division officially, while you nose around in the background". "Will you set the meeting up then?" I asked. "Already have" answered Bob, smiling as he reached for his coffee once again. He took a sip and put the cup down. "Thursday at 11.00 at Calgary, in a little café on 4 Street SW called Marty's Bistro". Bob then handed me the credit card and mobile phone. "They are both well in credit" he whispered. I took them and slipped them into my shirt pocket quickly, before anyone could notice.

We finished our lunch and walked outside together onto Preston Avenue. There was a nice breeze and the trees fluttered and swayed a little, their beautiful green and yellow leaves contrasted against the deep blue Saskatchewan sky. I wished that I was back up north, walking in the forests or by the side of a lake somewhere. Bob slapped me on the shoulder. "Go to it Billy" he said with a smile, "And stay in touch". He walked off down the Avenue and I walked back to where I had left Kanti. I could fly to Calgary from Saskatoon airport, but I strongly dislike flying, it always hurts my ears and then I would need some sort of transportation at the other end, so I decided I would drive. It's about 380 miles but the route is simple enough if I stick to highway no. 7 out of Saskatoon and then onto highway no. 9. I could stop at Drumheller for a break and to fill Kanti up before going on to Calgary. As this was Tuesday, I had plenty of time and decided to stay the night in Saskatoon at a little guest house I know on Lome Avenue, by the South Saskatchewan River. From there I could go for a nice walk in the evening and collect my thoughts. As I walked, I wondered why some people seem to be born with an evil streak. It serves no purpose. Can they not appreciate the wonder and beauty of the natural world around them? Can they not appreciate the wonderful heritage that we have in culture, literature, art and music? This world could be such a wonderful place if everyone was kind to the person standing next to them. Why hurt someone when you can comfort them and show them love? I can never understand why so many people allow greed to corrupt them and lead them down the path of evil. They will never be happy while walking such a path, as they will never understand what is really important in this precious life which we have been given. They will never abide with the Great Spirit or feel his warmth and wisdom in their hearts. However, I had to bring my mind to focus upon the case at hand, and it was certainly an interesting one, but with almost nothing to go on, except the body at Calgary. Perhaps Superintendent Penning could throw some light on the situation. But then, if that was the case, then why has this one remained on the unsolved list. That is unusual, especially when a Police officer has been murdered. Usually, such situations are strongly linked with the investigations being worked on and are solved quite quickly and decisively. I do not understand the criminal mind, but I must try to think like a criminal and place myself in their shoes. That is not an easy task. Still, I must try my best to assist in this matter.

3. Calgary

Kanti and I made the trip to Calgary and I arrived at Marty's Bistro a little ahead of the scheduled time and, after ordering a coffee, sat as far back as I could in the room. I liked to do this when meeting strangers as it gave me an opportunity to watch them as they approached. You can tell much by the way a man walks and looks in general; also by the way he addresses staff in little cafés and bistros. After a while, a tall man in a rather ill-fitting suit walked in, slowly and deliberately. He paused when he saw me and, after nodding to the waitress, came directly to my table. "Billy?" he asked, looking straight into my eyes with an open and honest gaze. "That's right" I answered, "Please, sit down Mr Penning". "You can call me George" he replied as he pulled up a chair and sat down. "I've been told that you have helped us on a few cases, sort of incognito?". I smiled and nodded gently. "Well, I don't know you at all" he continued, "but Bob Conwy seems to think that you might be useful to us in this instance, and I value his opinion".

“Thank you” I replied, “but we seem to have very little to go on in this case, other than the fact of the body being found in the Canadian Pacific engineering works. Do you think that there is a connection there?”. George Penning called the waitress over and ordered us a coffee, and then sat silently for a minute or two, as though turning something over in his mind. I did not interrupt, after all, I had no other appointments to go to, and this man seemed most interesting. Our coffees arrived and we sat silently.

George sipped his coffee. “You see” he started, very quietly. “I knew Roger since he was a teenager, before he joined the RCMP. He was the son of a friend of mine. So, I felt kind of responsible for him”. I said nothing, as I could see that the man was genuinely grieving for his lost colleague. “I trained him in basic detective work and he became very good. Very good indeed. His intuition was almost always correct”. George drifted into silence again. “Did he keep notes?” I asked. George looked up sharply. “Yes he did, and they were always clear and concise. He had been digging into a drug related operation here in Calgary and was obviously getting close to the source”. He sipped at his coffee. “So, what have we got?” I asked. George looked over his shoulder before continuing. “All I can tell you is that there are two private clubs up in the residential area of Mayland Heights. One of them is the Black Cat Club, run by a fellow named Nicolas Durand, up on Mariosa Drive”.

"And the other?" "The other is a very exclusive little place called the Orange Club, not too far away in Muray Place NE. This one is owned by Maxime Moreau, although he only visits it if there is some important business in the offing".

Now it was my turn to think silently for a moment. "Both French then, and in a nice part of the town, from what you say". "Exactly" confirmed George. "They are at the sharp end of the food chain and Roger thought that there was something very important about to happen". "And so they killed him" I suggested. "No, they had him killed. These guys run most of the hardened criminals in the city". George rose from his chair and, as he was turning to go, he paused. "One more thing, there was a word scribbled on the blotter on his desk; WRAAK. I have no idea what it means or what it refers to". With that, he pushed his chair in; "We shall not meet again Billy. You liaise with Bob Conwy". I watched as he walked slowly and deliberately out of the Bistro.

I finished my coffee and decided to explore the area around where the clubs were situated. Mayland Heights seemed an affluent area with some very nice houses and the odd, small office block dotted around and within them. I noticed some Doctor's surgeries and several Attorneys offices as well as one or two Real Estate offices. I drove along 8 Avenue NE and then down 19 Street NE until I got to Matheson Drive, then up Meota Road NE and left onto Mariosa

Drive. There were some nice houses, but one of them was particularly imposing with a large, black gloss door, upon which I could see a very small brass plate. Either side of the door were two white columns holding up a small porch above the door. I stopped Kanti a little further on and then walked back to the house. I stopped and looked from the pavement but could see no obvious activity and so decided to approach the door. As I grew near, the door suddenly opened, and a well built man in a dark suit informed me that this was private property. "I am looking for the Black Cat Club" I said confidently, adding, "Jacques recommended it to me, Jacques Perot". "I don't know any Jacques Perot" he said sternly. "Oh, that's a shame because I have come to do some business on behalf of my band". He looked me up and down. "You Indians are not in our league". "There is plenty of oil money now, together with shale gas concessions and other activities" I replied. He eyed me rather cautiously for a moment and then said, "Come back at nine". He then closed the door.

I had made my first connection and went back to my jeep and sat in it for a while to consider how I would take it from here. I had plenty of time before the evening and so went and had a look around downtown Calgary. Choosing one of the many restaurants, I went in and ordered a simple cheese salad and coffee. While sitting there, waiting for my order, two large men in smart black suits came in and sat at an adjacent table. They ordered some coffee and biscuits and then just sat, watching me attentively. They did not attempt to make contact, but it was clear that they were interested in me. I reasoned that they must have followed me from Mariosa Drive. Misiwanâpêw, I thought as I looked into their faces - bad man. I finished my meal and left to find an unassuming guest house that I could use as my base.

In the evening, I went back to the Black Cat Club, parking Kanti some way down the road and walking the rest of the way. I knocked on the door and, this time, was admitted by the same man that I had seen before. Inside, was a fairly large hallway, with various rooms leading off from it. Each had some activity or another going on inside it. I went into what seemed to be the most populated room and found a large roulette table with several people around it, some sitting and playing, others standing and watching. I made my way to it and stood next to a respectable looking man and woman. Before I could say anything to them, I was accosted by another big man in a dark suit. He pulled my arm so that I was facing him and said, rather purposefully, "We don't allow Indians in here pal". "I have come to see Nicolas Durand" I answered in a matter of fact way. "What do you want to see him about?" "Some business" I replied. "Come with me" the man said and I followed him out into the hallway where some other, identically dressed men were standing. “Throw this bum out” he said firmly and two of them manhandled me to the door and then outside, where they proceeded to attack me. I pushed one of them away, tripped the other up as he came towards me and then ran. Fortunately, I can run quite fast and would always rather avoid a confrontation than participate in one. I ran past the next house and then round the curve in the road that turns south. A quick glance confirmed that they were following me, so I jumped a fence and went back through the gardens, returning back to the Black Cat Club, my thinking being that this would be the last place that they would look for me.

From the back garden, I noticed that there was a door slightly open. I approached slowly and peered in through the gap. There was a lady washing glasses at a sink with her back to me. I opened the door quietly and sneaked past her and out through another door which opened on to a rear hallway. Here, there was a staircase leading to the upper floor and a quietly went upstairs to take a look around. I opened one door, which lead to a sumptuous bedroom, closed it again quietly and then opened another, behind which was a study. A large desk stood in one side of the room, with a green beige top and beautiful mahogany pillars. The top drawers were locked, but the two bottom drawers were not. In one was a concertina type of folder with assorted notes and letters stuck into it. In the other, a stack of unused envelopes, a hole punch, some assorted pencils and, importantly a key. I could see straight away that this key was not for the upper desk drawers, it was flat and rather small. Looking around me, I noticed a half height filing cabinet in one corner of the room. It was getting dark now and I did not want to risk turning on the light, but this filing cabinet was adjacent to the main window which had Venetian blinds. I opened the three drawer cabinet with the key. The top drawer had standard looking files, arranged in alphabetical order; A to C, D to F and so on. The middle drawer continued the series to Z. But the third drawer contained just one folder marked very clearly with the word MONTREAL.

I placed the folder on top of the filing cabinet, opened the blinds a little and started to examine the contents. There were one or two letters of little importance signed with the name Antoine. Some other assorted bills and then, a bunch of invoices with an address in Montreal at the top and signed sometimes by Antoine Laurent and sometimes by Clement Roux. I committed all of this information to memory, closed the blinds again, replaced the files, locked the cabinet and returned the key to the desk. As I was making my way out, I heard two people coming up the stairs, talking to each other. I darted quickly into another door which lead to a small bedroom, presumably for guests. Peeping out through the door, I could see that they had left the door to the study open and, if I were to walk past, there was a good chance that they would see me. I waited for a while, but there was no sign of them leaving. The small bedroom was in the front of the house and I reasoned that if I exited through the window, I could swing my legs over to the porch over the front door and then climb down one of the pillars. Providing the doorman was not outside, I should be fine.

I dutifully opened the window and lowered myself out with my waist over the ledge, before swinging my legs sideways and dropping down onto the porch. I climbed down one of the columns and was walking back down the drive, when a limousine pulled up outside and a very well to do couple climbed out and started up the path. I nodded to them and kept walking calmly out into the street. My previous assailants seemed to have disappeared and I made my way carefully back to Kanti. I turned around and drove back down Mariosa Drive in the opposite direction, so as not to pass the house. It had been a worthwhile visit as I now understood that the operation seemed to be being controlled from Montreal. That made sense, as they are close enough to the coast to receive shipments from merchant vessels, which are very difficult to police. I returned safely to my guest house and resolved the next day to visit the Orange Club in Muray Place. I felt sad for the people I was now mixing with. What were their lives?

They had a little money, but nothing else. Always looking over their shoulders and never enjoying the simple pleasures that a good life provides. Moreover, they understood nothing except avarice, violence, envy and hatred. That is no kind of life and to think that each one of these individuals was once someone's precious child who they once had hopes for. I had dinner and went to bed, where I was able to sleep contentedly.

The next day I made my way back to the Mayland Heights district and on to Muray Place, where I drove slowly up and down the whole street, but did not see anything that looked like a club. I decided to come back in the evening and park around half way along the road and just watch for who was coming and going. Soon enough, I noticed that expensive looking limousines were coming and stopping outside a particular house, their occupants entering into the establishment. I drove to the far end of the road and then walked back, observing the comings and goings at this house as I approached. This time, I went around the back of the house and found an open door which lead, via a short passage, to the main hallway where there were a number of people assembled. I was quickly approached by two men in dark suites who asked what I was doing there. "I have come to see Maxime Moreau" I stated calmly. The two men looked at each other. "There is no-one of that name here" one of them said, with which, they grabbed me by the arms and escorted me out of the front door. I went back around to the rear of the house and gently opened the back door again. This time, I avoided the main hall and went straight up the rear stairs. The upstairs of the building was deserted. I tried one door. It was locked. I tried another and entered into a reception room. There was a filing cabinet, which was locked, and a desk whose drawers were also locked. But on the desk was a tray containing some unopened envelopes. I picked them up and shuffled through them and, on the backs of two of them was the same Montreal address that I had seen at the Black Cat Club. It was an address in Rue de Rouen, in the Hochelaga district of Montreal. That was all I needed to know. The two clubs were both in correspondence with an address in Montreal which, in all probability, was supplying them with narcotics.

I returned to my guest house and called Bob Conwy to update him on what I had found. “So” said Bob, “It looks like there is definitely a narcotics operation operating out of Montreal and reaching at least as far as Calgary, if not further”. “Exactly” I replied, “And if they are using the railway for primary distribution, they can indeed reach right across Canada and even down as far as Kansas City in America”. We agreed that I would go to Montreal and nose around a little there, to see what else could be discovered. The next morning, I drove to Calgary station and booked my ticket on the Canadian Pacific for Montreal. The long train journey would give me time to think as well as avoiding air travel. Indeed, I enjoy travelling by train. I had a small compartment where I could stretch out and admire the scenery, while coming out from time to time to grab a coffee at the bar and watch my fellow passengers.

Once the big diesel electric locomotive (or sometimes two of them in tandem) started rolling, it slowly picked up speed and the golden fields started to fly by at the window and I entered into a different world. Thinking about how, by being inconspicuous and therefore able to go places that the RCMP could not, at least, not so easily, I was able to help them start putting the pieces of this narcotics ring together. However, there was still something that did not seem to fall into place. Something was missing and, as the big train rolled along, I became more convinced that it was something to do with the Canadian Pacific network. But what? At the moment, it was not clear. Anyway, on to Montreal.

4. Montreal

The train rumbled on, south to Regina, where it stopped for twenty minutes or so, as new passengers joined and others disembarked for the Capital, and then onwards it rattled towards Winnipeg. I joined the train in the late afternoon and now the light was fading, throwing shadows across every feature outside. Others in the train began to settle down, as they usually do when night is approaching. I sat down and, as I often do, wrote a little verse which would guide me along my way for the next few days.

Something good is coming in the night
Passing swiftly through the stars
And out into the morning light
Bringing comfort from afar

So close your eyes and drift away
And think of all that you hold dear
And all those worries that held sway
Will all fly far away from here

Let the morning fill your heart
With love and joy for everyone
Let it find a brand new start
A new tomorrow has begun

The train arrived at Winnipeg in total darkness and, once again, there were some who joined and some who left. But soon, it was on its way towards Thunder Bay, Sudbury and Toronto, which it would reach in the early morning. And then, north east up to Montreal, where we arrived just before lunch.

The first task was to establish a base and I found an unassuming guest house on the Avenue du Midway, right there in the Hochelaga district where the address I had was based. After a shower and change of clothes, I had a light lunch in a nearby café and then set off to find this address in the Rue de Rouen. It was a shipping agent. That made sense, I considered as I observed it from the other side of the road. However, there seemed to be very few clients going back and forth. I decided to investigate.

I pushed open the heavy door and walked up to the reception desk, behind which a man sat in shirt sleeves, smoking a cigarette. On the desk, an ash tray betrayed his habit of heavy smoking. He looked up at me with a questionable look, but didn't actually say anything. "I would like to see either Antoine Laurent or Clement Roux" I asked, in a matter of fact way. "I am Antoine Laurent, what do you want?" he replied.

"Well, I had heard that I might be able to set up a little business with you, you know, on behalf of my reserve". "I don't know what you are talking about" he replied bluntly. "If you want to ship something somewhere, just say so". I thought on my feet. This man was obviously not going to give anything away. "Actually, I was expecting a parcel to be delivered here from Paris" I said quickly. "Name?" he asked. "Devereaux" I said. He looked through his system. "Nothing of that name". "Perhaps I could take a look?" I asked. "If it was here it would be on the system" he replied angrily. "OK, merci bien" I replied and left through the heavy door. I looked at the other businesses on that block. There was a clothing store, a large book shop and a car parts store, among others. I thought it likely that they all had rear access to storerooms of one sort or another.

At the end of the block, I went down the adjacent street and, indeed, found a narrow driveway running behind the row of stores and businesses on Rue de Rouen. I walked slowly along and, about where the shipping agent would be, there was a medium sized truck unloading some parcels. I walked slowly past and observed the legend on the truck, it was; 'Enterprise Clement Roux. Marine Marchande'. Yes, this was definitely the place. I walked slowly past the truck and then doubled back, squeezing myself between the front side of the truck and the wall. I watched the men unloading the parcels and, while they were not watching, I slipped into the little warehouse and made my way silently to the far side, where I sat down behind some large crates, out of sight of the main activities going on just a short distance away. I reasoned that, if I wait until they finish work for the day and leave, I will then be able to investigate further.

I sat for what seemed like hours. I looked at the edge of the crates and imagined shapes like animals. I thought of Pinehouse Lake. Oh how I wished I was back there, walking by the endless shoreline and watching the sun glint off the surface of the water as it sat down slowly in the west. I longed for the comforting sound of howling wolves and, instead, heard the vulgar chatter of working men making crude jokes. Eventually, their day ended and they pulled down a large metal shutter over the entrance to the loading bay and secured it with two bolts, one either side. Then, a sliding gate was drawn across and a large padlock fixed to secure it in place. I peeked round from behind the crates and saw the men climb up two steps and exit through a plain looking wooden door. As they did so, one of them turned off the light and I was left in darkness, except from a crack of light coming from the partly opened door. They chatted and laughed for a while with Antoine and then I heard them go. A little while later, the door was pulled to and locked and then, a minute or so later, I heard the slam of the front door. I waited for a few more minutes in order to be sure that I was alone on the premises, and then turned on my pocket torch and began to investigate.

There were various boxes and packages strewn about, including some on a table which looked like they had been repacked ready for shipment. In the corner there was a cage containing a around twenty or so parcels, each about 35 cm square. The cage was secured with a large security padlock. I shone my torch over the parcels and, on some of them, could see some franking marks with the word 'Marseilles' emblazoned upon them. I selected the larger knife blade from my pocket toolkit and, through the mesh of the cage, slid it into one of the parcels near the edge, so that the cut would not easily be noticed. On drawing the knife out again, some white powder came with it, some sticking to the blade. I knew immediately what it was. Cocaine. I went back over to the table where three packages had recently been prepared. Two of them were labelled with an address in Winnipeg and one was addressed to the Black Cat Club, in Mariosa Drive, Calgary.

So that was it. They were importing the drugs from Marseilles and redistributing them from Montreal, no doubt via the Canadian Pacific network. I jotted down all the relevant information in my pad and then went across to the wooden door. It was a relatively crude device, fitted roughly into a frame of 6 x 6 cm timber. The slant of the bolt was on my side of the door and, on sliding my knife into the gap, I was able to spring the bolt backwards and unlock the door. It lead into a small room which was like a kitchen, with another leading off from it to the side which was the bathroom. On the opposite side from the door was another, half glazed door, the glass being opaque. It was not locked. I opened it gently and found myself back in Antoine Laurent's office. The Venetian blinds on the exterior windows were not quite closed and that on the door was only pulled down halfway. I moved over quietly and gently closed the blinds so that the light from my torch would not be seen.

The drawers on Laurent's desk were not locked and there were assorted documents of no particular interest. An adjacent filing cabinet was also not locked and there were various records of, presumably legitimate, transactions. In the third drawer was a folder marked 'Marseilles' and, in it I found invoices from an address in Orange Avenue, Marseilles, with the names Raphael Morin and Dorian Boyer on them. I made a note in my notebook.

In the bottom drawer, behind the folders, was a cardboard box. I opened it and, inside, were a number of small papers, each one of which had the word WRAAK and a date written on it. I remembered that George Penning had mentioned the word WRAAK back in Calgary. Also in the box was a business card from a law firm named Gabrielle Romano and Associates, on the Boulevard Saint

Laurent, here in Montreal. As I sat there at the desk, I could feel the spirit of maci in that room. How could any human being make a living out of the abject misery of others? I had heard that even children were being targeted at schools and were becoming addicted. Many teenagers had died horrible deaths by using bad quality merchandise and many more would no doubt do so. Yet more would have their lives ruined by addiction to these awful substances, while those peddling them became obscenely rich in the process. I just wanted to get away from that place as soon as I could. I replaced everything carefully, put the blinds back as they were and then let myself out of the front door. As I did so, an alarm went off. I pulled the door closed behind me and walked away briskly, but not so fast as to attract attention. People would no doubt just consider it as another false alarm.

The next day, I found the law firm on Boulevard Saint Laurent, just opposite Parc Jarry, but there was no Gabrielle Romano, as I soon found when asking the receptionist. "We only deal with private clients here" she said icily. On an adjoining glass door were the names Pierre Fournier, Florian Girard, Guillaume Dupont and Bastien Garnier. "But I am a private client" I insisted while noting the names. "In any case, Bastien Garnier was recommended by a friend". The receptionist stared at me for a moment and then picked up the phone. "There is someone here asking for Mr Garnier" she drooled. "You may go in" she indicated with a nod towards the door. I went inside to find two men, one sitting behind the desk and another standing behind him. "Sit down" said the man behind the desk. I did so and noticed a waste paper basket to one side of the desk, about midway along its side. "Well, what do you want" the other man said. I looked at their faces, in order that I might remember them. "I wish to find a missing person" I said calmly. "Who sent you here?" said the man behind the desk. "Oh, someone in a bar suggested that you were the best lawyers in town" I replied. The man behind the desk suddenly became aggressive. "You're lying" he shouted and the other man came round behind me and grabbed me by the shoulder. I feigned a coughing fit and bent over in my chair. "Get up" shouted the man behind the desk. I reached into the waste paper basket and quickly grabbed some of its contents and pushed them into my trouser pocket as I stood up, still coughing loudly. I have found that, if coughing, all attention seems to be upon your face and, consequently, my grab of the waste paper had not been noticed. "Get out of here" shouted the other man, as he pushed me, quite violently, towards the door. I did not argue, but went out through the reception and the front door, back into the street. I turned and looked back at the door, to find one of the men standing there with his arms folded, in a defiant pose. I crossed the road and went into Parc Jarry. Towards the other side of the park, I sat on a bench and slowly pulled out the screwed up papers from my pocket. One was a letter confirming an appointment, from no other than Clement Roux. The other had that word WRAAK on it again, with a date, roughly two weeks hence and the numbers 9359 and 9375.

I found a local library and looked through some dictionaries and thesaurus volumes but could find no reference to the word WRAAK. I asked one of the librarians for assistance. “It sounds like Dutch to me” she said after considering the problem for a moment or two. After searching the shelves, we eventually found a Dutch to English dictionary and, she was quite right. The word ‘wraak’ in Dutch means ‘vengeance’ in English. It was time to head back to Saskatoon.

4. The Drugs Ring

The next morning, after breakfast, I checked out of my guest house in Montreal and went straight to the station, where I purchased a compartment ticket for Saskatoon. The train was scheduled for just after lunch, so I had a snack at a nearby café and ran over the situation in my mind. I had discovered a good deal here but felt that Montreal was, for me, an evil place. I would be glad to leave.

Back in the station and, eventually, the train rolled in from Albany, clanking and hooting its horn. I boarded and went straight to my compartment, where I closed the door and watched from the window. Around fifteen minutes later, whistles were blown, horns sounded and I felt a slight tug as the big train started to slowly pull away. For the first time in a while, I was kamiyawâtamihk, happy to be leaving this miserable place. I lay down on the bench and closed my eyes for a while as the train picked up speed and fell into a gentle rhythm of clanking along the track, albeit very quietly. I thought more about the events of the past few days. It was clear that there was a well ordered drugs distribution with the substances coming in from Marseilles and being processed by the shipping agent in Montreal before being shipped across the country, probably using the Canadian Pacific network. After all, it was perfect for the task, stopping at every major city, from Montreal to Vancouver and even reaching down into North America. The law firm, I imagined, would be managing the finances. That too was a good front that no-one would immediately think to question. Yes, it was well organised, but there was *still* something else nagging away at me and it had something to do with the railway. I took out my pad and wrote;

Who forsake all that they've learned
The tenets of humanity
No matter what they think they've earned
Such closed eyes shall never see

The truth as its laid out ahead
The beauty all around to see
The loving words that may be said
And all the good that may yet be

For those whose hearts are closed and dark
No light will ever come to shine
No joy will ever leave its mark
But witness still the march of time

I then closed my eyes and drifted away. It was a long way to Saskatoon after all. When the train stopped at Thunder Bay, I went to the dining car and ordered some coffee. I got talking to a stranger who was travelling on to Edmonton. “Its amazing how many travel on this route” he continued, “Whatever time of day or night I travel, the train is always close to full”. I asked him if this was the case all along the route. “Pretty much” he replied, “Certainly from Winnipeg to Vancouver, and often right from Montreal”. It turned out that my friend was a travelling salesman who promoted specialist magazines and journals. I thought carefully about what he said. If the Wraak collective was some sort of terrorist group, then a train might be an obvious choice to hold people ransom or even commit an atrocity of some kind. I determined to thrash out this possibility with Bob Conwy when I reached Saskatoon. The nagging in my head was becoming both more pronounced and a little clearer now. I was convinced that there was more to this than a simple drugs ring.

The train clanked and whistled its way through Winnipeg and onto the last, long stretch to Saskatoon. The dawn broke and the sight of the golden wheat fields lifted my heart as the train sped along the tracks, taking me to my home Province.

Upon reaching Saskatoon, I booked into my usual guest house and called Bob straight away, indicating that I had a great deal to impart to him. We arranged to meet at the Redlands Café for lunch, where we could enjoy one of Grace Billing's famous omelettes. I had a shower and placed most of my clothes into the washing basket at the guest house, just as I had done at Montreal, then, donning the last of my clean shirts, I headed off for a leisurely walk towards Preston Avenue and the Redlands Café.

Unusually, Bob was there before me and nodded towards me from the back table. I came and sat down, followed closely by Rosie, who was keen to take our order. That task accomplished, I pulled out my notebook and confirmed the names and places that I had already given Bob over the phone, but added what I had gleaned from the lawyers and the translation of the word 'Wraak'. "So you think that the Gabrielle Romano law firm is really running the show" suggested Bob. "I do" I replied, "But I do not think it is just the drugs ring. I believe that this activity is being used to raise funds for something else". "What exactly?" asked Bob. "I don't know yet, but I am convinced that it has something to do with the railway and that that is why Roger Smythe was murdered. I think his investigations were starting to touch upon the larger organisation. Certainly, he had discovered something about Wraak". Bob sipped his coffee and thought for a moment. "With a coordinated effort across the RCMP we could move in on them all at once" he suggested. "We have enough on them now to certainly convict them on a narcotics rap". "I know" I replied, "But I think we should wait until after July 14th", which was the date on the paper that I had intercepted. "You think there is something big going to happen on that day?" "I think that there is certainly something planned for that day and, if we move in now, they will simply postpone it and we shall have lost the thread". "So what do you suggest?" asked Bob. "Let me go back to Calgary and work with the local RCMP there" I suggested. Our omelettes had arrived and Bob said nothing for a while and then announced, "I shall have to clear it with Stuart Grant and Bill Tavistock in Regina" he said before taking another sip of coffee, "But I agree with you in principle". "OK, I shall wait to hear from you. I am at the usual place" I replied. We finished our meals and, after a few pleasantries, went our respective ways.

As I was walking back to my guest house, it occurred to me that July 14th was Bastille Day in France. I wondered whether this was significant. It could be if our Wraak friends really were a terrorist group. By the time I reached the guest house, I had a strong sense of destiny, as Indians often do, and knew that I must go to Calgary without delay. Bob already knew that I would go, with or without the approval from Regina. It was just a matter of timing. Besides, I had to go back, as Kanti was still sitting there in the car park. She would be missing me by now. Consequently, as soon as I arrived back in my room, I called Bob again and told him that he could contact me in Calgary, and reminded him of the guest house that I stayed in the last time I was there. Then I collected my clothes together, packed everything in my bag and checked out of the guest house.

Walking through Saskatoon to the station, I thought of how I would much rather be up at Pinehouse Lake, walking along the banks under the starlight with the big Tipiskāwipisim watching over me from above. Or maybe, early in the morning, fishing with my friend John White Stone, where, with hardly a word being spoken, we would enjoy the quiet companionship which comes with the years. More likely, I would be talking with the wild animals in the forest and feeling privileged to be a part of this fleeting picture of nature. I love the north. But it is endangered now by the discovery of minerals and fossil fuels. I pray to Misimanito that nature prevails and keeps this beautiful land as it should be. However, my priority now is Saskatoon Station.

6. Vengeance

The man at the ticket window eyed me warily as I booked my one way compartment ticket to Calgary. He had no idea who I was or why I was travelling there late in the afternoon, but displayed a mixture of curiosity and suspicion none the less. It did not worry me. I needed neither his approval or permission to be travelling in my own country.

It was early evening before the train rolled in, with lights flashing and horn blowing, like a big red dragon, towing behind it a trail of carriages. I boarded and eventually found my allotted compartment, right at the end of one of the cars. I put down my bag and sat on the seat and watched from the window as everyone scurried about, getting ready for departure. After some more horn blowing, I felt a slight judder and heard the clanking of the wheels on the tracks, slowly at first, but then gradually picking up speed as we set out for Edmonton and then, after changing trains, down to Calgary. The light was slowly fading and, on some of the curves, I could see out of the window, a beautiful red sunset just beginning to build, with a purple sky surrounding it. How wonderful nature is. I wonder how many eyes have gazed lovingly upon such a sight. Not just humans, but animals too, as they most certainly have a sense of the aesthetic, just as they have emotions and feelings. I love them more than I do humans. They are more reliable and they never forget a friend.

However, for now, I must turn my attention to this business in Calgary. I closed my eyes and thought intensely of the wraak organisation and those four names at the law firm, Pierre Fournier, Florian Girard, Guillaume Dupont and Bastien Garnier. Hopefully, through Bob Conwy, the combined forces and offices of the Royal Canadian Mounted Police would attach some background to these characters. It slowly, but very definitely, came to me that they were indeed planning a terrorist attack of some kind for July 14th. It was also inextricably linked to the railway. I sat, with my hands upturned on my knees and my back straight and let my mind wander wherever it chose. It chose darkness for a while and then, quite suddenly, an image came to me of a big red locomotive running at speed along the track. Was it just self-suggestion because I happened to be on a train at that moment? No, I don't think so. This was a very clear premonition of something in the future. But what? I would have to let my intuition guide me in Calgary and see what I could discover about this dreadful business. Time was not on my side and I would have to work quickly if anything was to be exposed and countered.

I eventually arrived in Calgary in the early hours of the morning and, after waiting for some time in the station, made my way to the familiar road and checked in at the same guest house where I had previously stayed. It wasn't long before Bob contacted me and advised that the various RCMP departments would be following up on the information that I had provided, although no arrests would be made until after July 14th, excepting in the event of discovering a terrorist plot, in which case, they would move immediately. I understood their position and advised Bob that I would see what I could uncover here in Calgary.

My first stop was to revisit the Canadian Pacific Engineering Works where George Penning had arranged for me to speak with their head of Engineering, Edward Wilson. Ted was extremely helpful and offered his full support to my enquiries. "If there is anything being plotted on one of our trains, I want to know about it" he confirmed as we walked to the main engineering hangar. Ted showed me the inside of a typical locomotive and even allowed me to drive it on the siding, so that I could get a feel for how it operated. The controls seemed straightforward enough; a throttle with numbered positions, a two stage braking control and ancillaries such as the horn and flashing lights controls. In addition, there were two small screens with information about the locomotive being displayed, some rudimentary dials and a telephone with which the driver was always in direct communication with the operational control centre.

We returned to the main hangar and, upon my request, Ted had an engineer remove some of the panels in the cab to reveal the electronics. There was a myriad of wires, leading in every conceivable direction, together with a black box to one side and into which various connectors made contact. “What does that do?” I asked “That’s the Locotrol system” volunteered the engineer. Ted explained. “When we have two or more locomotives in tandem, the Locotrol system distributes power and braking control in order to obtain the best efficiency”. “But what would happen if it went wrong?” I asked. “Then it would automatically fall back to a fail-safe operation and revert to manual control”. “And if it did not?”. “Then the driver can turn it off completely and take over the controls”. I asked to look inside the Locotrol box and the engineer removed the screws from the cover and pulled it off. Inside was a large circuit board with several plug-in connectors which, in turn, connected to the external inputs. It was an extremely complicated looking affair and, immediately, my intuition told me that this was a vulnerability that could be exploited by someone with the necessary knowledge. Other panels were removed, but all I saw was a mass of wiring and various conduits leading off to other parts of the locomotive.

Ted then showed my the passage that led down one side of the locomotive, enabling drivers to be switched or take a rest in one of the cars during a long journey. From this passage, other panels could be removed which gave access to the engine. This was done with a special hexagonal key and the engineer showed me how it was done. The engine itself was very impressive, with a turbocharger and exhaust recirculation as well as a complex fuel injection system, all driving a giant alternator which provided the electronic power.

The pieces of this puzzle were beginning to assemble themselves in my mind. I was now convinced that there would be some sort of an attack on one of the trains on July 14th and that it would likely be on the locomotive itself.

Back in Ted's office, I asked him if I could have one of the keys used to remove the engine inspection plates. I did not have a rational reason for asking, but I somehow knew that I would need one. He had one sent up from the works, together with the square key used to open the interconnecting doors of the locomotives and I attached them all to my key ring. "By the way Mr Wilson, do the numbers 9359 and

9375 mean anything to you?". He looked puzzled for a moment. "They sound like locomotive numbers" he suggested. He turned on his desk chair and logged on to a computer screen. I sat quietly and patiently while he navigated his way through various sections. "They were delivered a couple of years ago" he exclaimed. "And where are they now?" I asked. He did some more checking. "Well, what do you know" he said quietly, "One of them is right here in the siding, awaiting a minor service". "And the other?" I asked. He did some more checking. "It is currently in Winnipeg, awaiting a trip to Toronto". I asked whether he could tell from his system where every locomotive would be on a particular day. "Of course" he said proudly, "But we shall have to go to the Ops room to see that".

The Operations Room was extremely impressive, with the whole route displayed upon a giant screen and dozens of smaller screens showing various items of information. Ted spoke with the Operations Manager, Sue Becker, and asked her if she could ascertain where the two engines would be on July 14th. She approached one of her staff and, together, they made several queries on one of the computers, before printing out a single sheet of paper. "There you are" she smiled as she handed the paper to Ted Wilson. He looked at it carefully. "Now that is interesting" he said quietly, "The two locomotives will be operating in tandem to pull a combo train from

Toronto to Calgary on the southern leg via Regina. "What's a combo train?" I asked. "A combination of passenger and freight" Ted replied. "More and more of our business is freight now, in fact, there are suggestions that we shall become a freight only company soon".

I thanked Ted and Miss Becker and drove down to the Inglewood Wildland Park, where I could walk among more natural surroundings and think. I was missing Pinehouse Lake and the Bridgewater Reserve and even thought about driving back there so that I could walk by the lakeside once more and let my intuition have free rein. However, there was no time for that now, so the Inglewood Park would be the next best thing.

The fact that these two locomotive numbers were known to the Wraak consortium suggested that they also knew where these engines would be on July 14th. Certainly, they were the target of some sort of activity. Could it be that they would smuggle their own drivers on board the train at the last minute? But then what purpose would that serve, other than being able to stop the train wherever they pleased? No, it had to be something more than that. Could it be that an explosive device would be planted on one or other of the locomotives? That might be a possibility, but it would have to be very well concealed if not to be found, and that would suggest collusion with the Canadian Pacific engineers. Still, it was a possibility that needed to be checked and each locomotive would need to be very carefully inspected prior to the journey. Perhaps an explosive device would be established somewhere along the track. That was a perhaps a more realistic possibility as such a device would be impossible to locate, given the length of track involved. However, somehow, I was not inclined towards the explosive device idea. After all, as Bob had said, such a device could be planted at a station or within any public building or area. No, it had to be something else, and something directly related to those two locomotives.

I sat in the sunshine with my palms upturned on my knees, closed my eyes and let my mind wander wherever it chose. Once again, I had a vision of a big red locomotive running very fast along a track. But nothing else. I stayed in the park until late afternoon and then drove back toward my guest house. I was low on fuel and Kanti coughed and spluttered a little until I found a service station at which to fill her. As we pulled up the slight incline towards the pumps, she juddered a little, and my thoughts immediately returned to those Locotrol boxes. They effectively controlled the motion of the whole train. It must be something to do with them.

Having filled Kanti's tank to the brim, I continued my journey to the guest house and partook of their evening meal before retiring to my room. I telephoned Bob and was informed that some background had been found on those names that I had uncovered and that all of them had been in trouble of one sort or another, and some actually had served terms of imprisonment. The situation did not look good. These were desperate men who had no respect for the law or, by definition, for society itself.

I laid down on the bed and continued to juggle the various possibilities in my mind. Clearly, the passage of the train in question was going to be interfered with at some point. How serious this interference was likely to be, was hard to tell, but the fact that an underground consortium was involved, the Wraak organisation, suggested something very serious indeed. If there locomotives were not to be blown up, and I did not think that they would be, then a derailment would seem a possibility. But then, they would not need to concern themselves with the locomotives to achieve such an end. That could be brought about by a simple manipulation of the tracks. No, something was definitely being planned for those two locomotives.

And then it came to me. My visions of speeding trains suggested trains out of control. I thought again of the Locotrol system and reasoned that such a system would be the obvious target for malicious interference. But they would need to have an expert available to achieve this. They must have either a Canadian Pacific or General Electric engineer under their control. Someone who has not yet been identified. The situation remained unresolved and time was running out. It was already July 11th. We needed to make some important decisions, and act upon them.

The next day, July 12th, after an early discussion with Bob, I called again on Edward Wilson at Canadian Pacific. I told him frankly of my suspicions and asked his advice on how we could best protect those two locomotives. He walked up and down in his office for a while and then, leaning on his chair, said thoughtfully, "We will have both locomotives checked from head to tail in Toronto, and the operation will be supervised by some of my own team from here. There will be no possibility of getting any untoward devices on those locos". "Right" I replied, "And, with your permission, I will set off now for Toronto and will ride in the front compartment of the train". "I will get you a special pass and have it ready to collect at the station" replied Ted. He looked at me, as though still not really knowing what to make of me, and then came up and slapped me on the shoulder. "Do your best for us Billy" he said with a smile.

I quickly collected some things from the guest house and then drove straight to the station and booked a compartment for the first train headed for Toronto which, by chance, was also taking the southern link. That was useful as it would afford me the chance to become familiar with this part of the track, as it headed off in a south-easterly direction before joining the main route to Regina and then on to Winnipeg, Thunder bay, Sudbury and Toronto. I seemed to be spending a good deal of time on trains, one way or another, but this was appropriate, given the situation. On this trip, before darkness set in, I explored the other coaches and looked for obvious spots where someone might plant an explosive device. There were plenty, but I considered that, in all cases, such a device might soon be spotted. I sat at the bar and ordered a coffee. While drinking it, I gently observed some of my fellow passengers, a variety of business types and casual travellers. No one spoke to me, but that is how I like it, ka kâmwâtahk.

I arrived in Toronto just after lunch on July 13th and immediately checked the schedule for the train that we were interested in. I was just in time, as it was leaving just after midnight. I had a sandwich and cup of coffee at the little café on Front Street West, adjacent to the Union Station, and then, having collected my special pass, made my way to the platform.

7. The Train

I sat on a bench on the platform, listening out for announcements and waiting patiently for the train. Others slowly started to populate the platform and I scrutinised them closely, although not knowing what, in particular, I was looking for. But sometimes I get a feeling when a bad person is close to me. However, on this occasion, I had no such feeling. Everyone looked perfectly normal and relaxed. Looking out through the glass panels beside the far tracks, I could see the bright lights of Toronto, with huge buildings reaching up to the sky and the highway running along at the bottom with yet more bright lights coming and going. I sighed and thought how much I disliked cities and yearned to be back home. However, I had an important duty to perform and nothing would prevent me from doing so.

After what seemed like a very long wait I saw the twin flashing lights of the leading engine approaching and heard a distant horn blow. The long train moved closer and closer, with the two locomotives coming almost to the very end of the platform. They were a mightily impressive sight. Like two red giants getting ready to haul this long train through the kaleidoscope of ever changing Canadian scenery to its eventual destination. The train stopped with much clanking and, from the passenger cars, steps were dropped down in order that passengers could board. I watched them do so for a while before I boarded myself. No one appeared in the least bit out of the ordinary and, eventually, I climbed the steps myself and entered into the first compartment in the first car.

For a while, I looked out of the window, but there was little to see. Just the other tracks and a confusion of lights in the distance. How things must have changed since they built that Union Station with its magnificent stone halls, which are now interspersed with electronic sign boards. I was thinking that this must be one of the busiest railway stations anywhere and would surely make a better target for some sort of terrorist activity than a train. But still, I was convinced that it was the train that was the target. We waited for around twenty minutes and then, with much whistle blowing and horn blowing, I felt the initial shudder as the wheels started slowly rolling and we drifted out of the station. For quite some time, we moved slowly through the suburbs of Toronto, before starting to pick up speed as we headed, north west, out of the city and on to the main track, occasionally passing though small towns as we made our way towards Sudbury. Although it was night, I remained wide awake, anxious to notice any little deviation from the norm. I walked up and down through the passenger cars, buying a coffee at the bar and bringing it back to my compartment. All seemed straightforward with no sign of anything suspicious.

Eventually, we rolled into Sudbury and the train slowed normally, coming to a gentle halt in the night. A few additional passengers joined the train and I got out, ran to the front of the leading locomotive and gestured to the driver. He gave me the thumbs up sign and I returned to the passenger car, just in time, before the station porter started blowing his whistle. I started to wonder whether I had been mistaken about the whole thing and that, maybe, there was going to be no attack on the train after all.

As we headed out west toward Thunder Bay, the dawn started to announce its coming with a gently diffused light coming from somewhere behind us. It grew a little more intense as the blackness in front of us changed to a velvet blue and then, lighter and lighter until the fields and farms became quite discernible, like pastel drawings. After a few hours I started to see that magnificent lake out of the left hand windows of the car and stood in awe, mesmerised by its beauty and scale. It roused a feeling in my heart that made me yearn even more for my own Pinehouse Lake. How wonderful Mother Nature was in all her creations. Not just all creatures, great and small, but the fabric of the Earth itself. Its mountains, valleys, deserts, rivers and lakes and all of the associated ecosystems. This, after all, is the *real* world, a beautiful world which we should be at pains to protect and preserve at all costs. Sadly, it looks as though we shall continue to ignore this reality, so long as there is money to be made by its destruction.

We stopped at Thunder Bay and I was tired now, having not slept much for the past twenty four hours or so. But not too tired to notice two official looking men is suits climb up into each locomotive and then exit again a couple of minutes later. I wondered who they were. Canadian Pacific officials perhaps. Or maybe even law enforcement officers from the RCMP, checking that everything was all right. While collecting my thoughts, whistles were blown again and the big train started pulling slowly away. Well, everything looked as though it was going to plan so far. Or was it? No one had mentioned these men to me. I sat and contemplated the situation.

8. The Runaway

After around fifteen minutes, it occurred to me that the train was travelling faster and faster. A few miles out of Thunder Bay, there is a right hand curve as the train heads north west up the track. We were travelling fast now, the scenery rushing past more quickly than it should have been. Twenty miles or so along and the track turned to the left and headed due west. As we took the curve, the whole train heaved over in a most alarming manner and I could hear the passengers becoming nervous about this, with much clamouring and questions being asked.

Using my special key, I went from the leading car, across the linkage and opened the back door of the rear locomotive. Moving through the passageway, I opened the adjoining door to the cab and there, slumped in his chair was the lone 'driver' who was supposed to be keeping an eye on the various screens and dials of the locomotive. He had been killed. Shot at close range with a hand gun, probably fitted with a silencer. Now I understood what those men is suits were doing back at Thunder Bay. I suddenly thought of the driver and co-driver in the front locomotive. Scrambling out of the main door of the engine, I held grimly to the hand rails as I swung myself out to the very front of the locomotive. Somehow, I had to cross the coupling between the two and enter the back door of the front loco. The train was rattling along very quickly now and swaying from side to side on the track. Not feeling confident to simply walk across the coupling, I got down on my hands and knees and crawled slowly across, lifting myself up on the other side by a connecting pipe of some description. I managed to open the rear door and made my way quickly through the passageway and into the cab.

Both men were slumped in their chairs, both killed in the same manner, with a bullet in the head. I leaned over one of them and grabbed the phone in order to communicate with central operations control. The line was dead. I reached in front of the driver and moved the throttle lever to the zero position. It made no difference at all. I remembered the Locotrol box and, with some difficulty due to the presence of the dead driver, managed to remove a panel and inspect the box. I took the cover off hurriedly and looked inside. As far as I could remember, it looked no different to the one I inspected at Calgary. The train swayed and heaved as we took another right hand curve and I wondered how it was staying on the tracks. The connections entered the Locotrol box via screwed junctions and I tried removing them one by one, but to no avail. The train kept hurtling along. I looked for other connections, such as the main throttle, but whatever I tried to disconnect, nothing happened. A sharp left hand curve and the train lurched once again to one side. Now it was a straight track all the way to Winnipeg and the train was gathering even more speed. I knew that after Winnipeg, there were a series of sharp curves and that, at this speed, the train would struggle to negotiate them.

I tried the brakes again. Nothing. I looked for cables coming from the brake levers, but it was all electronics and everything seemed to disappear into a rats nest of cables, leading off in every direction. There was an emergency brake. I tried applying that, but nothing happened. By now we were approaching Winnipeg station and it occurred to me that, if the central control did not know of the situation as yet, they soon would do. No doubt the passengers would, by now, also be greatly agitated, but I would have to leave that situation to the staff on the train.

I sat on the floor behind the drivers seat and thought about the situation as calmly as I could under the circumstances. If all the electronic controls had been bypassed and there was no easy way of restoring them. Then there must be a mechanical way of stopping those big engines. All I had was my multi-purpose tool and small flash-light. Hardly an engineer's toolkit. Still, I must try to do *something*. As I stood up, I saw Winnipeg station hurtling towards me and had the presence of mind to find the horn button and give a long blast, in order to clear passengers from the track. The train continued at a frightening pace as I moved into the passage at the side of the locomotive. I started removing the inspection panels as quickly as I could, hoping to see something obvious that I could control. There were cables attached to the big engines but, as had already been explained to me in Calgary, these were mainly telemetry sensors which fed back information to the on-board computers. I ripped a few off anyway, but nothing changed. Suddenly, we hit the curves outside of Winnipeg and I was thrown sideways against the bulkhead.

Picking myself up, I realised that there was only one thing for it, I would have to climb in, on top of the engine and somehow try to disable it. However, the distance between the inspection apertures and the engine was too small for me to climb through. I started to bend and rip away the steel panels at the most promising looking spot, but it was still impossible to get into the engine bay. They must do it somehow, when servicing these beasts, I reasoned. But then I remember seeing in the engineering works, locomotives with their roof panels removed. The inspection bays within the passageway simply enabled rudimentary checks to be undertaken. I sat down and thought for a moment or two. The train lurched violently from side to side as we hit some more curves on route to Regina. No, there was no other way, I had to get into that engine bay somehow.

I persevered and, after more bending and ripping and with my hands bleeding, managed to squeeze the top half of my body, backwards against the hot engine. Getting my arms inside the engine bay, I grabbed hold of some pipe or other above me and hauled my body inside, managing to get a foothold on one of the open inspection hatches and push myself upward and onto the top of the huge twelve cylinder engine. As I did so, I heard a commotion both outside and coming from the rear of the train, including some police sirens. Evidently we were tearing through Regina station.

I was, by now, extremely tired and weary and could hardly think straight, and then I remembered. The very sharp right hand curve that would normally take the train sweeping up towards Calgary. There was no way that a train travelling at this speed could negotiate that curve. It would certainly derail. My thoughts clearing, I realised that I had to stop this engine. There were various cables that I wrenched out from their sockets, but all to no avail. Then, I realised that if I could cut off the fuel supply, the engine must stop. I looked at the aluminium pipes which carried diesel to the injectors on each cylinder. I followed them back with my eye, hoping to see a single junction that I could disconnect, but they all swept downward toward the rear of the engine and there was no time left for me to go crawling around down there. I would simply have to sever each one of them in turn.

It was burning hot and uncomfortable on top of the engine, but I rolled over in order to get to one side of the vee and, after selecting the saw blade attachment of my tool, started to saw through one of the pipes. It broke easily enough and diesel was being pumped out all over both me and the engine. I continued to do likewise with the other five on that side and could feel that the engine was running very rough. I, however, found myself almost swimming in diesel. I rolled over in the vee of the engine and repeated the procedure on the other side. As I broke through one pipe after another, the engine became rougher and rougher, the inertia was keeping it turning for a while and, while it was turning, the big alternator was generating power. Of course, I also had to disable the second locomotive.

I managed to extricate myself from the engine bay and, soaked in diesel, rushed out of the passageway and negotiated the coupling between the two engines once again. It was more difficult in reverse as there was less to hold onto on the front of the locomotive. I finally managed to get inside and rushed straight through the cab and into the passageway. This time, I only removed the inspection hatches that I knew I would need to in order to get into the engine bay. It was difficult. I was tired and my hands were slippery with a mixture of diesel and blood. Finally, I managed to squeeze in and get on top of the second engine.

It was with great relief that I noticed that the train was already travelling a little more slowly, but still much to fast to safely negotiate that curve. After all, it had picked up a great deal of momentum now. I twisted around to face one side of the vee and my multi-purpose tool slipped from my hand and rattled down deep into the vee of the engine. I tried pulling and twisting the pipes but, with my slippery hands, this was not working. I needed my saw blade.

After much difficulty I finally managed to retrieve the tool and started frantically sawing away at the pipes. One, two, three, they started breaking apart and spraying me with even more diesel. Four, five six and then rolling over for the other side. The diesel was getting everywhere and stinging my eyes as I continued to sever the fuel pipes. Finally, the last one broke and, for a few moments, I lay helpless on top of the engine, completely exhausted. I felt the engine turning ever more slowly and clattering as it went. The train was also slowing down, although, without brakes and with plenty of momentum behind it, it was still travelling quite quickly. I took a few deep breaths and wriggled my way out of the engine compartment. I thought it best to get back up into the cab of the front locomotive, in order to sound the horn if and when necessary. I managed to get over the coupling again, through the passageway and into the front cab. I gently pulled the driver from his seat and sat down at the now useless controls. I sounded the horn a couple of times, thinking that it might reassure passengers who, by now, would realise that the train is slowing.

As I sat there, exhausted and squelching with diesel oil I watched the track advancing towards me inexorably. In fact, the train was still travelling at quite a speed. A crossing loomed up ahead and, to my horror, I saw cars going across the road. I gave several long blasts on the horn and, thankfully, the cars stopped as we approached. A little later, the strong right hand curve appeared and the train rattled on around it without issue and continued on its way. I wondered if it was ever going to stop. However, a couple of minutes later, it finally ground to a halt, some miles away from Calgary.

Immediately, a couple of police helicopters came and landed in a field next to the track, and a number of armed officers rushed out and climbed up into the cab. “Oh, am I pleased to see you” I exclaimed. “Likewise” said one of the officers as he looked at the dead bodies of the train drivers. Before I knew what was happening, I was bundled off of the train and held fast by the arms by two officers. Meanwhile, some police cars were bouncing along the dirt track at the side of the field and some more armed officers came bursting out of the cars and ran to where we were. “He’s all yours” said one of the flying squad and thrust me towards the other officers who, despite my protestations that I had just saved the train, handcuffed my hands behind my back and bundled me into the car. We then sped off, presumably towards Calgary.

9. Back to Saskatchewan

"I am not who you think I am" I protested, "Could you please radio ahead and ask to speak to Superintendent Gorge Penning. Give him the name Billy and mention Bob Conwy and Stuart Grant at Saskatoon. He will know the meaning of this". "All in good time fella", replied one of the officers. "But we haven't got time. This is important - please make the call". The officer who was in the back seat of the car with me looked at me angrily, "Don't tell us our job Hiawatha". I laughed and said that I would not tell him his job, but that this is important as immediate action needs to be taken. "George Penning will understand this immediately" I added.

The officers continued to ignore me. I could not really be angry with them, after all, how were they to know what had been going on. We eventually reached the police station where I was searched, my belongings removed and thrown into a cell. "I am allowed to make a phone call" I shouted as they disappeared down the hall. After what seemed like an age, a police sergeant arrived and I explained to him calmly that, actually, I was working undercover with the police and that urgent action was needed. I repeated my plea to contact George Penning or Bob Conwy. "Look" I said, "I am allowed to make one phone call, please bring back my phone and I will call Bob Conwy in front of you and then you can speak to him". The sergeant looked at me for a moment. "Come with me" he beckoned, and we went to an interview room where, finally, he called Bob Conwy. After a moment explaining the situation, the sergeant handed me the phone "he wants to speak with you". I grabbed the phone. "Bob?. Is that you". "Yes, what's going on Billy, I have seen the train on the news". "I will explain all later Bob, but I've a feeling that we should move quickly and arrest all those who we know of", I explained. "The wheels are already in motion Billy, we knew something was wrong when the train didn't stop at Winnipeg. But what about you? Are you all right?". I chuckled, "Well, sort of, but I would appreciate my bag being brought up from the train so that I can have a shower and a change of clothes, I am soaked in diesel at the moment, and you know what that does to the skin". "Let me speak with the sergeant again" said Bob. The sergeant took the phone and, after a moment or two, looked round at me in astonishment. "Right, we'll do that right away Sir" he said and then replaced the receiver. He looked at me and smiled. "I'm sorry Billy. We had no idea that you were on our side all along". "I tried to tell you" I replied with a smile. "Not to worry, come with me and we will loan you some clean clothes until your bag arrives". We went to a locker to grab some police clothing and I was then shown into a shower room. At last, I could remove some of the oily grime that had seemed to have worked its way into every pore.

Coming out of the shower, dressed in a police uniform, I was given a nice cup of coffee and shown to the staff room where I could relax in comfort until my bag arrived. The door opened, and who should walk in but Superintendent George Penning. "Leave us if you will gentlemen" he said, and the two or three others who were in the room quietly left. George smiled and shook my hand "Well done Billy, we might still have been in the dark had it not been for your undercover work". "Thank you Mr Penning" I replied, "I always knew that it would be something to do with the train. I had a heck of a job stopping it though" I grinned. "I'll bet you did" he laughed, "Those locos are not designed to be easily stopped". George looked at me with a serious expression on his face. "I am sorry that the officers did not believe you" he said sympathetically. "That's OK" I replied, "They cannot believe what they are told by every Tom, Dick or Harry. It is not their fault". "Is there anything else you need?" he asked. "No, just my bag and then I will change and be on my way back to Saskatoon" I replied. "You should stay in that uniform. You might like it here" quipped George. "No thank you" I said sincerely, “I prefer it up at Pinehouse Lake”. George Penning nodded and quietly returned to his office.

After a while, my bag arrived and I changed into my own clothes and checked that I had all my belongings, especially my keys. With all being in order, I made my farewells to the station staff and one of them gave me a lift to the station car park where I picked up Kanti. Turning the key in the lock and climbing in behind the wheel, I heaved a sigh of relief. It was all over. Except, of course, that I would have to give a full report to Bob Conwy and Stuart Grant in Saskatoon. I turned the ignition key and Kanti sprang into life, eager to embark upon another long journey. She must have been mightily bored sitting there all this time.

I took a leisurely drive back, on the same route I had used before, stopping off for a break and fuel fill up at the same place and eventually arrived in Saskatoon in the early hours of the morning. I stopped at Kinsmen Park, where I could walk across Spadina Crescent and sit by the banks of the South Saskatchewan river. It was a good spot to watch the dawn break and make me think about who I was and why I was engaging in this strange activity. It had something to do with a sense of belonging. I am Cree and my people go back a very long way on this land. But I am also a Canadian, and proud to be one. I must therefore do what I see as my duty for both communities. We must stand up to those who would pervert our land and our country, no matter who or where they are. And I, as a citizen of this country, have a responsibility in this context, even if I do prefer to stay up in the north, away from the big cities and their bright lights. I looked into the waters of the river and smiled. “Ah, Mistahi-sîpîhk, Nitôtêm” I whispered, and bent down to touch the cool waters of the early morning. The great river had seen everything, from before the first of my ancestors arrived, to the current day. And she would still be running after we have all gone from this place.

As soon as they were open, I drove to the police station to meet with Bob Conwy. We both went into a meeting room where there was a secretary and also Chief Superintendent Stuart Grant. Bob and I went through the whole story of how we uncovered the drugs ring. “Have they all been arrested now?” I asked. “The Montreal division are taking care of that at their end, and we have those in Alberta” answered Bob, “also we are working with Interpol to nail the Marseilles end”. We went on to the train journey itself. “It was at Thunder Bay that the big change was made” I began, “Two men is suits climbed up into the cab of the rear locomotive and then exited a couple of minutes later. The same must have happened for the front loco. They were the killers and somebody must have seen them at the station” I suggested. “Probably contract killers” suggested Bob. “But they must have known how to flip the Locotrol system like that” I reminded him. We looked at each other for a few moments and then Bob said what we were all thinking. “There must have been some sort of collusion with the engineers at the Canadian Pacific works. We will follow that up, but your job is done Billy”. It was then that Stuart Grant spoke. “How on Earth did you manage to stop those engines Billy”. “Well, it was not easy” I replied with a smile, “It involved getting on top of those big diesels and cutting through the fuel line to the injectors”. “Ha!” he laughed.

When all was done and I was about to depart, Bob grabbed me by the arm. “Not so fast Billy”. He said with mock seriousness. “You and I are off to lunch at the Redlands Café, that’s the least we can do”. “Quite right” retorted Stuart Grant, and Bob and I drove in his car to Preston Avenue. We walked in the half empty Café and Bob called out, “Two of everything Gracie” to the owner, who smiled and said simply, “Right away”.

We enjoyed a quiet lunch, talking of the various cases we had worked on together and then Bob gave me a lift back to the station to pick up Kanti. We shook hands and I climbed aboard my car and sighed. So, that was that. I turned the ignition key and headed north.

10. Back to Pinehouse Lake

I drove off up route 12 and then on to route 55, where I stopped for a while at Big River. I filled Kanti up and we continued, right up, past Green Lake and Beauval before swinging off east and then north to Pinehouse Lake. It was still dark when I arrived, in the early hours of the morning. I parked as quietly as I could and walked back through the forest, on the trail that led to the edge of the lake. I continued around the banks for a while until I found a little clearing, and there I sat and rested. Home at last.

What an adventure I had had. However, I cannot tell the details to my aunt Marie as she would worry about me. She knows that I help the police, and that is all she really wants to know. I laid back and watched the fading stars as the sky started to get ready for another day. I heard something rustling behind me and looked back to see the familiar silhouette of a large black bear. “Ah, come on maskwa, come on sweetheart” I said softly. She came a little closer and waved her head from side to side, as though uncertain. “Come on maskwa, you have seen me a hundred times before. You know me” I continued, speaking quietly and radiating that unspoken communication that all children of the forest understand. She came right up to me and pushed her nose into my chest, as I sat there, before lifting her great head and looking straight into my face. “You beautiful creature” I said quietly and stroke the side of her neck. She turned and sat down beside me, and there we were. Betty maskwa, as I had named her, myself and Misimanito, all sitting together and watching as light slowly rose from the east and a mist sat over the still waters of my beautiful lake. Slowly, the mist itself cleared as the sun rose slowly and a new day had begun.

I breathed slowly, but deeply, drawing in the clean air of the north. This was the land that I loved, and from which I never wish to be separated. There is nothing that money can buy that I need. I thrive on the love that exists here all around. The love of the natural world and all the creatures, large and small, which make it all work. I can here the chattering of red squirrels and the sound of birds singing their morning greetings. I slowly got to my feet. “Its time for me to go now maskwa” I said quietly, and retraced my steps back through the forest trail and on to the Bridgewater Reserve. I let myself into the house as quietly as I could but, naturally, aunt Marie was wide awake and waiting for me. “You should not have got up for me aunt" I suggested. She smiled. "I knew you were coming five hours ago" she replied, as she busied herself getting some coffee ready. Of course she did. They always know. Cree women have a sixth sense in that respect and often predict important events as well as knowing when visitors are coming.

We had some coffee and toast and, seeing that I was tired, aunt Marie suggested that I went to my room and rested. I went and laid on my bed and thought about the events of the past few weeks. Why are some men bad? They are not born bad, surely? A new born baby is not an instant criminal. Perhaps it is the experience of early childhood that makes them that way. But to be prepared to actually kill others, strangers that you don't even know. That is just kâmacatisihk. How could they not appreciate the value of life? That precious gift that all creatures hold for just a short time on Earth. We all have a duty to enrich that spirit, before passing it on, beyond the sky to the great pool. Those who waste their time with greed and maliciousness, can never understand the beauty of life. And it is there. All around them, if they care to look. Me? I have everything I need here on the Bridgewater reserve. And more. Within walking distance, I can visit the wonderland of the forest. The big trees that have stood there for generations are like friends as I pass them on the trail and on to the lake. Here I can sit by the still waters, close my eyes and become the man that nature intended me to be. I maintain my own code of living, just as the other creatures of the forest do, and I respect life, and the natural world from which we have all sprung.

Maybe, one day, I will get a communication from Bob Conwy again, asking me to help them in some way or another. Maybe not. Whatever the future holds, I shall follow the path ahead of me, and follow it with truth and with love. Maybe, I will meet with you somewhere along the trail?

Kisipipayiw

Printed in Great Britain
by Amazon